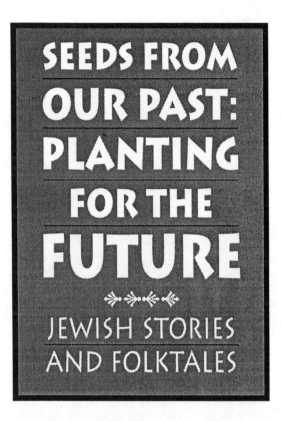

SEEDS FROM OUR PAST: PLANTING FOR THE FUTURE

❖❖❖

JEWISH STORIES AND FOLKTALES

EDITED BY CORINNE STAVISH

B'NAI B'RITH CENTER FOR JEWISH IDENTITY
WASHINGTON, DC

Book printed in the United States of America
Printing: Todd Allan Printing
Graphic Designer: Howard Israel Bullard
Illustrations: *Medieval Life Illustrations,* New York: Dover Publications, Inc., 1996
Cover design: Howard Israel Bullard
Production Coordinator: Sandra Wiener

Library of Congress Cataloging-in-Publication Data

Stavish, Corinne, Editor
Seeds from our past, planting for the future: Jewish stories
and folktales.
p. cm.
ISBN 0-910250-31-6
1. Legends, Jewish. 2. Jewish parables. 3. Hasidim - Legends.
4. Jews - Folklore. 5. Tales
BM530,B474 1997
296.1'9–dc21   97-36375

For Nicole and Scott, my first audience.

"...and you shall teach them diligently unto your children, and shall talk of them when you sit in your house, and when you walk by the way..."

<u>Deuteronomy</u>, 6:7.

Louise —

May all your days be filled
with wonder and stories,

Connie
Stanish

CONTENTS
OF SUBJECTS/THEMES

FOREWORD

he Center for Jewish Identity (CJI) is proud to present this compilation of Jewish stories and folktales. We hope that the contents of this book will encourage and enrich communication within your family and your community.

Stories have a special magic. The power of a story can be found in its simplicity and its ability to combine a fable, an allegory or a moral within that story. Stories can jar our conscience. They focus on and preserve our culture, values and history. Stories make our teachings relevant; they serve as a tool to deal with the truth.

The Aggadah tells us that King Solomon invented and used stories as parables for the writings of the Torah. Rabbi Haninah compared the Torah to a well of cool, fresh water. Because the well was so deep, no one could get to the bottom of it. King Solomon, through his parables, gave people the rope they needed to reach that bottom.

Throughout history, when a situation seemed hopeless, stories have remained a constant source of inspiration. They provided people with a usable format that is still employed today. Teachers, counselors and people on all levels use stories to teach ideas, to preserve events or to make a point. Stories serve as both a comfort and a tool to maintain our Jewish culture and identity.

Storytelling itself is an art form and we are fortunate to have such a fine artist as Corinne Stavish in our CJI family. Corinne has trained our staff in storytelling techniques; she has also served as the editor of this book. It is both a pleasure and a privilege to work with her.

I am sure you and your family will find great meaning and inspiration while reading these Jewish stories and folk-tales.

Ofra Fisher
Executive Director
B'nai B'rith Center for Jewish Identity

INTRODUCTION

SEEDS FROM OUR PAST: PLANTING FOR THE FUTURE

magination is more powerful than knowledge, and nothing challenges, stimulates and produces imagination more than story. An old Jewish tale recounts how Truth was walking down the street one day, naked. People ran away from her, uncomfortable, frightened. Parable approached Truth and gave her some advice: "People shun you because you are naked, bare and plain. I am similar to you, but I dress myself up so that I am more pleasing to behold. Why not try that?" Truth did, and from that time on, Truth and Parable have been inseparable friends, revered by everyone, the foundation of stories.

In our stories we find essential human relationships and truths. They are our collective human conscience and consciousness, the teaching instruments used by rabbis and sages for millennia. Jewish stories reflect our social, religious and human values. They are our cultural his/story. However, since Jews never created anything in a sealed environment, much of our folklore reveals some form of cultural exchange and interchange, supporting its continued breadth and applicability.

Dov Noy, Director of the Israel Folktale Archives (IFA), reminds us that: "Whereas the universal folktale appeals to the present psychological state of the listener, delighting him with a pat resolution that is a formalistic happy ending, the Jewish folktale is future-oriented urging the listener to adopt an ideal or goal as yet unrealized, to improve his ways and change his attitudes." In other words, Jewish stories urge us to go beyond what we think our limitations may be. Jewish stories offer challenge and hope. Jewish folklorist and author Howard Schwartz affirms that in the Jewish story ... "an implicit moral is present, as well as, a reaffirmation of faith."

If stories have such power and possibility, then we must use them with our children of all ages. Stories frequently help us to identify and to understand our problems more clearly. They are seeds we plant now whose fruits will nourish future generations. (See "The Figs" page 41.) Minimally, they help us to talk about issues. The stories in this volume are intended to be trigger stories, used to stimulate discussion. (They may also be read and enjoyed without organized discussion). Discussion means a dialogue whose purpose is to exchange ideas, not to preach and moralize. Effective dialogue frequently produces more questions than answers. Productive dialogue results in real listening (understanding as well as hearing). Constructive dialogue is always conducted with respect.

Therefore, it would be a disservice to the integrity of these stories and to the purpose of the Parent/Teen Dialogue program or an informal family dinner "table talk" to tell someone what the story means. In the Appendix (page 81) of this volume is a Discussion Guide to aid parents, teachers and facilitators who wish to use the stories in a structured way.

These tales are organized by obvious themes for easy use. However, each listener will find new and different subjects that the story may address. As with the introductory tale (page 15), which has become storyteller Penninah Schram's signature story, one may "shoot first, then draw the circle."

Most of the stories in this collection are taken from anthologies of Jewish stories, (though many stories appear in other cultures). At the end of each tale, the specific source is cited when copied directly. However, where I reworked stories from several sources or retold one that I had only heard, it says, "retold from traditional sources." Since the primary audience for this book is parents and facilitators, I do not detail the etymology of the stories. This collection is not a scholarly work, does not pretend to be, and clearly relies heavily on more prestigious sources. For careful and thorough analyses of the history of many of these stories, readers should refer to Penninah Schram's *Jewish Stories One Generation Tells Another,* any of Howard Schwartz's marvelous works, and Ellen Frankel's *The Classic Tales: 4,000 Years of Jewish Lore,* all listed in the bibliography. These three authors shine as scholarly contributors to Jewish folklore.

Both Penninah Schram and Howard Schwartz have influenced my development as a storyteller, and I thank them. Also, I applaud Ofra Fisher's vision for this book and Sandra Wiener's relentless work on its details and graphic choices. Ellen Singer's assistance, including the inspiration for the title, in the last few weeks of the project was helpful.

Stories were our first form of communication. Today they can be used to enhance communication and to trigger discussion. Because stories have no boundaries, we feel no limitation in ourselves as we listen. We perceive our internal strengths and possibilities. Myth becomes more powerful than fact, imagination more powerful than knowledge. Stories endure. Take them; use them; plant them. Through them, we can find Truth, for no clothing can conceal her.

Corinne Stavish
August, 1997

ACKNOWLEDGMENTS

he stories in this collection that were not retold by the editor, were used with permission. We appreciate the cooperation of the following publishers and authors and list the works we use from their publications.

Bialik, Hayim Nahman and Yehoshua Hana Ravnitzky, eds. *The Book of Legends, Sefer Ha-Aggadah.* New York: Schocken Books, 1992.

"Noah"

Board of Jewish Education of Greater New York. *101 Jewish Stories.* New York: BJE, 1961.

"Banquet in Heaven"
"No Respect"
"Praying with a Flute"
"The Alphabet"
"The Figs"
"The Dishonest Carpenter"
"The Finder's Reward"
"The Magic Ring"
"The Princess and Rabbi Joshua"
"Two Brothers"
"Two Humble Men"
"You Can't Please Everybody"

Lewis, Shari. *One Minute Jewish Stories.* New York: Dell Publishers, New York, 1989.

"The Honored Garment"

Pavlat, Leo. *Jewish Folktales.* Prague: Greenwich House; distributed by Crown Publishers, 1986.

"Gold and Iron"
"The Fox As Advocate"
"Vengeance in Vain"

Rush, Barbara. *The Book of Jewish Women's Tales.* Northvale: Jason Aronson, 1994.

"The Bird and Her Three Goslings"

Schram, Penninah. *Jewish Stories One Generation Tells Another.* Northvale: Jason Aronson, 1987.

"Wine to the Wedding"

Schwartz, Howard. *Gates to The New City.* Avon Books, 1983.

"The Prince Who Thought He Was a Rooster"

SHOOT FIRST

he Maggid of Dubno had a vast repository of stories that he called upon frequently. Once, a student was walking with him and asked, "How is it that no matter what the occasion, you always have a story that fits?"

"I'll tell you a story," the Maggid of Dubno replied.

A soldier returned from a war and went through a small village. On a wall at the edge of the village, he saw hundreds of circles with bull's-eyes shot accurately—dead center. Because he considered himself a superior marksman, he wondered who in this tiny village could achieve such accuracy in target practice. The soldier spent the day searching for the marksman. He discovered that it was a young boy. He took the boy to the edge of the village and showed him the wall, covered with bull's-eyes.

"Did you do that?" he inquired.

"Yes I did," replied the lad.

"I don't understand how," said the soldier. "I am a superior marksman, and I cannot hit the target with 100% accuracy. How do you do it?"

"Actually, it's pretty easy," announced the boy. "You see, I shoot first, then I draw the circles."

"So it is with my stories," said the Maggid. "I have many stories that I tell. When I want to tell one in particular, I merely direct the conversation to that subject, and tell the story."

Retold from *A Treasury of Jewish Folklore* by Nathan Ausubel and *Jewish Stories One Generation Tells Another* by Penninah Schram

THE OLD JEW AND THE NAZIS

 n elderly Jew in Berlin finds himself surrounded by a group of raucous Nazis, who knock him to the ground and ask him, derisively, "Jew, who is responsible for war?"

The little Jew is no fool. "The Jews," he replies, "and the bicycle riders."

"Why the bicycle riders?" ask the Nazis.

"Why the Jews?" counters the old man.

Retold from traditional sources

GOLD AND IRON

ne day Gold set out into the world. It walked until it arrived at a place where it could hear a terrible sighing and wailing. "What can that be?" said Gold to itself. It went closer and saw a gorge, where a blacksmith was striking a piece of hot iron with a great hammer. At each blow Iron groaned, and there was no end to its suffering.

"Why do you lament so?" Gold asked Iron. "All metals are beaten—even I, Gold, have the same fate. Men long for me, but I am struck just as you are."

"How can you compare our fates?" sighed Iron bitterly. "I am a metal, as you are, it is true, but there is a difference between us. You are beaten by iron, not gold, and it is quite usual to suffer at the hands of strangers. But I am struck by my own brother, and that is a pain worse than any other."

From *Jewish Folktales* by Leo Pavlat

BUILDING BRIDGES

here once were two young men who were the best of friends, the very best of friends since childhood. The young men did everything together. They worked together; they played together; they studied together; they even thought together. One young man could start a sentence and the other young man could finish that sentence. They spent most of their waking hours together and never tired of each other's company.

As they grew older and approached manhood, they each decided to leave their families and build homes of their own. They found a wonderful spot near a lake where they had spent many wonderful hours fishing. Ah, they imagined how wonderful it would be to be neighbors. And so it was that they built their houses on opposite sides of the lake. They would wake up early in the morning, row out to meet one another and fish for hours on their lake, spending even more time together.

One morning as they were fishing and talking, talking and fishing, they had a mild disagreement. This was most unusual for the young men because they never disagreed about anything. They became confused and uncomfortable. How could they not agree with one another? The more they discussed, the more they disagreed, and suddenly they were really angry with each other, and both rowed back to their homes.

One young man was so angry and confused, that the more he looked across the lake at the person who used to agree with everything he said and used to agree with every-thing he did, and used to be his friend, the more upset he became. Finally, he called a carpenter and told the carpenter to build a tall fence around his house so that he would not have to look out of his window at that horrible person across the lake.

The carpenter went to work immediately. The young man went into his home, content with the rhythmic sound of the hammering of the carpenter. Finally the hammering stopped, and the carpenter invited the young man to see the finished work. Out went the young man, expecting to see a fence. What did he view? It was a **bridge** spanning the lake! The man was so angry at this total disregard of his instructions that he failed to see his former friend come running across the bridge from his end of the lake. Then, he stopped yelling long enough to notice his former friend waving his arms and shout-ing his praises as he rapidly approached.

"Thank you, thank you. You are so wise to have seen what a ridiculous quarrel we had, certainly not worth the loss of our very special friendship. "Thank you for building this bridge so I could get here quickly to say please, forgive me. I was wrong." "No, it was my fault," replied the friend. They laughed as they almost began to argue over who was to blame.

Then, they turned to the carpenter to thank him and invite him to stay. The carpenter smiled, gathered his tools, and said, "I must go. You see, I have many more bridges to build."

Retold, based on a story by Pleasant De Spain

NOAH

hen Noah began planting, Satan came, stationed himself before him, and asked, "What are you planting?"

Noah: "A vineyard."

Satan: "What is its nature?"

Noah: "Its fruit, whether fresh or dried, is sweet, and from it one makes wine, which gladdens a man's heart."

Satan: "Will you agree to let both of us plant it together?"

Noah: "Very well."

What did Satan do? He brought a ewe lamb and slaughtered it over a vine. After that, he brought a lion, which he likewise slaughtered. Then a monkey, which he also slaughtered over it. Finally a pig, which he again slaughtered over that vine. And with the blood that dripped from them, he watered the vineyard.

The charade was Satan's way of saying that when a man drinks one cup of wine, he acts like a ewe lamb, humble and meek. When he drinks two, he immediately believes himself to be as strong as a lion and proceeds to brag mightily, saying, "Who is like me?" When he drinks three or four cups, he immediately becomes like a monkey, hopping and giggling, and uttering obscenities in public, without realizing what he is doing. Finally, when he becomes blind drunk, he is like a pig, wallowing in mire and coming to rest among refuse.

All the above befell Noah.

From *The Book of Legends, Sefer Ha-Aggadah,* edited by Hayim Nahman Bialik and Yehoshua Hana Ravnitzky

FISH AND SNAKE

nce there was a little fish who left her school and was swimming around. Her parents had told her never to go too close to the shore because there lurked many who would try to tempt her out of the water. But, it looked so pretty near the shore that one bright, sunny day, she swam very close to shore.

A snake happened by and said, "Little fish, little fish, come out of the water. I have something special for you."

"I mustn't do that," said the fish. Remembering what her parents had told her, she swam away, calling, "No!"

But the snake kept insisting, "Oh please. I will give you special things to make you feel ssssso good."

"I already feel good," said the fish. "No!"

But this was a persistent snake. "Oh come on, you don't know until you've tried," said the snake. "It could be quite pleasant."

"Well, said the fish, "that's true."

"So come on out. You'll see marvelous things you've never seen before."

"Well—I really should say no!"

"But," said the snake, "it will be a new experience."

"Well, maybe tomorrow," said the fish.

The next day, the fish swam near the shore again. The snake was waiting. "Come on little fish, try it, just once!"

The fish did not say no; she didn't even think it. She was really tempted to try something new. She swam very close, and as she was about to leave the water, she noticed many dead fish in the sand. Just at that moment, the snake uncurled herself and made a leap for the little fish, who ducked and escaped and swam away.

"You see, snake," the fish said, "I can't possibly have better experiences on land, because it's not safe for me there, and you know that. I just won't even try that. No, I won't. I'm going to stay where I belong and have a chance of being safe." And the little fish went back to her school.

The snake stayed there on the shore, waiting for some foolish fish to show up. Many did; many thought that the snake's offer would bring fun, only to end up tasting poison.

The fish may not have lived happily ever after, but she lived for quite a long time, and she had fun too.

By Corinne Stavish, inspired by a Rabbi Akiva story

YOUNG MAN IN THE FOREST

nce, there was a young man who went into a forest. He walked most of the day. It grew dark; the young man looked for a way out of the forest, but he could find none. He spent the night in the forest, cold, hungry and frightened.

The next day, the young man began to search again for another way out of the forest. He went down many paths, but no path led him out. He spent another night cold, hungry, frightened, and now discouraged.

The third day, the young man again searched the many paths to find one that would lead him out of the forest. Still, he found none. Then, suddenly, he saw an older man walking towards him. The older man was dressed as if he belonged in the forest.

Rushing to him, the young man shouted, "I'm so glad that I have found you. Thank goodness that you are here. I am lost, and no path I follow leads me out of the forest. Please, help me!"

The older man smiled: "How long have you been lost in the forest?"

"Three days," replied the young man.

"Then why are you so upset? I have been lost for three years."

"Oh no," cried the young man, completely discouraged. If you have been lost for three years, then it is certain that we will never find our way out."

"No, no—not at all," said the older man. You see, although I do not know which path leads out of the forest, I know all the paths that do not."

Retold from Hasidic sources

THE BIRD AND HER THREE GOSLINGS

 mother bird had three goslings. When the season for migration arrived, she took the first gosling and carried him on her back to bring him to a warm land. When they were over the sea, the bird asked her gosling, "My son, when you grow up and are strong, and I am old and weak, will you take me to a warm country?"

"Of course, Mother," answered the gosling. The mother bird snatched him from her back and sent him to the sea.

She returned and carried the second son. And when they were over the sea, she asked him, "My son, will you take me to a warm land when I am old and you are strong?"

"Of course, Mother," answered the second gosling. He too was taken from her back and dropped into the sea.

Then the mother bird took the youngest gosling from her nest and carried him on her wing. And when they were over the sea, she asked him, "My son, when you are big and strong, and I am old and can no longer fly under my own power, will you carry me on your back and deliver me to a warm country?"

"No, Mother," answered the third gosling, "I will not be able to carry you, for then I will have to carry my own goslings."

The mother was happy with her son's answer and delivered him to a warm land.

From *The Book of Jewish Women's Tales* by Barbara Rush

NO RESPECT

nce upon a time, a very rich man was ailing and aging. So he called his only son and said: "My son, I am growing old and I find it difficult to run my business myself anymore. You and your wife are very energetic and intelligent people. I will give you all my cattle and sheep, and you and she will take care of them. You will not have to wait until I am dead to achieve prosperity."

The son kissed his father, thanked him for his kindness, and promised to take care of him. He gave his father a fine room in his house and a servant to take care of his needs. And his ventures prospered. When a son was born to him, the young man was full of joy. The mother thought of nothing but the son's future and how to ensure that he would have much money set aside for him when he grew up. Thinking this way, they grew very selfish and stingy as they tried to save money.

Little by little, they denied the old man more and more. At first, they took away the old man's attendant, and then they took away his room. By now, they had grown very rich, and they invited many fine guests to their home. They were ashamed to have the poor old doddering man sit down at their fine table.

"You have spilled your soup over everybody, idiot!" the wife would scream at him, in front of all their fine guests. "You belong in the stable!" And indeed soon they made room for him there.

But even that place was soon taken away from him, for their cattle and horses had grown so numerous that they needed every bit of the stable for them. The old man was flung into one corner stall, among the rags and rubbish. He was by now forgotten and neglected by almost everyone.

But one person did remember him. That was the little grandson. He would go each day to visit his grandfather. He had to do this secretly, for his mother would not let him go in his fine clothes to that filthy corner of the stable. She would scream at him, and at the old man if she knew that the grandfather had kissed and embraced him. She would have thought it an even worse crime that the boy returned his kisses and embraces and that the child clasped loving arms around the ragged grandfather.

One day, the father saw his son playing some strange game using two heaps of blankets. He hurried over for a few minutes to play with his little boy. He could not afford much time for him nowadays, because he was too busy making a lot of money.

"What are you doing there, my son?" asked the father.

"Well, I take a pile of blankets from the house and I place them in this heap. And then I take the rags and rubbish out of the miller's cellar, out of the kitchen, and what is left over from the horses' bag of oats, and I pile them in this pile."

"And why do you call this game 'Father and Son'?" he asked the boy.

"Oh, I'm the son and you are the father," said the boy. "And I am saving these rags for you when you get old like grandfather, and these rich and expensive blankets I shall keep for myself so that I can always be warm and happy."

Then the man awoke to what he had been doing to his own father, and he kissed his son and thanked him for having opened his eyes to the terrible sins he had been committing.

From *101 Jewish Stories*, New York Board of Jewish Education

THE REBELLIOUS CHILD

abbi, Rabbi," shouted the father, rushing, child in his arms, into the rabbi's chamber. "You must help me to discipline this child. He is constantly rebellious and disobedient. I get so angry with him that I grab hold of him and shake him. Sometimes I hit him. Still, he does not obey me. Can you help me? Tell me, what should I do?"

"Oh yes, I can help" replied the rabbi. "You must certainly use physical force with him. I recommend that you grab hold of him, take him close to you, and hug him long and hard. Continue to hold him and to hug him, and do not ever stop."

Retold from Hasidic sources

THE PRINCE WHO THOUGHT HE WAS A ROOSTER

nce there was a prince who fell into the delusion of thinking he was a rooster. He took off all his clothes, sat under the table, and refused to eat any food but corn seeds. The king sent for many specialists, but none of them could cure him.

Finally, a wise man appeared before the king, and said: "I think that I can cure the prince." The king gave him permission to try.

The wise man took off his clothes, crawled under the table and began to munch on corn seeds. The prince looked at him suspiciously, and said: "Who are you, and what are you doing here?"

The wise man answered: "Who are you, and what are you doing here?"

"I am a rooster," answered the prince belligerently.

"Oh really? So am I," answered the wise man quietly.

The two of them sat together under the table until they became accustomed to each other. When the wise man felt that the prince was used to his presence, he signaled for some clothing. He put on the clothing, and then he said to the prince: "Don't think that roosters can't wear clothing if they want to. A rooster can wear clothes and be a perfectly good rooster just the same."

The prince thought about this for a while, and then he too agreed to put on clothes.

After a time, the wise man signaled to have food put under the table. The prince became alarmed and he said: "What are you doing?" The wise man reassured him. "Don't be upset. A rooster can eat the food that human beings eat if he wants to, and still be a good rooster." The prince considered this statement for a time, and then he too signaled for food.

Then the wise man said to the prince: "Do you think that a rooster has to sit under the table all the time? A rooster can get up and walk around if he wants to and still be a good rooster." The prince considered these words for a time, and then he followed the wise man up from the table, and began to walk.

After he began dressing like a person, eating like a person, and walking like a person, he gradually recovered his senses and began to live like a person.

Written by Rabbi Nachman of Bratslav, translated by Jack Reimer, published in Howard Schwartz's *Gates to the New City*

THE TWO BROTHERS

ong ago, on the site of Jerusalem, the holy city, there lived two brothers. They were farmers who tilled the land they had inherited from their father. The older brother was unmarried and lived alone. The younger brother lived with his wife and four children. The brothers loved each other dearly and did not want to divide the fields between them. So together they plowed, planted, and harvested the same crop. After they cut the wheat, they shared equally the produce of their labors.

One night during the harvest, the older brother laid down to sleep. But his thoughts were troubled. "Here I am," he said to himself, "all alone, with no wife and no children. I don't need to feed or clothe anyone. But my brother has the responsibility of a family. Is it right to share our harvest equally? After all, he needs more than I do!"

At midnight he arose and took a pile of sheaves from his crop, carried them to his brother's field, and left them there. Then he returned home and slept in peace. That same night, his brother also could not sleep. He was thinking about his older brother. "Here I am," he thought. "When I grow old, my children will take care of me. But what will happen to my brother in his old age? Who will take care of him? His needs are greater than mine. It isn't fair to divide the crops equally!" So, he arose and took a load of sheaves, brought them to his brother's field, and left them there. Then he returned home and went to sleep in peace. When morning came, both brothers were amazed to find their crops exactly as they had been the night before. They wondered how such a thing could happen, but did not speak to each other about this strange event.

The next night each brother repeated his actions of the previous night. When morning came, again they were amazed to find they had the same number of sheaves as the night before. But on the third night, when each of the brothers was carrying a pile of sheaves to the other, they met at the top of the hill. Suddenly, they understood. They dropped their sheaves and embraced, weeping with gratitude and happiness.

The Lord saw this act of love between the brothers and blessed the place where they met that night. And when in the course of time King Solomon built the Temple, from which peace and love and brotherhood were to flow to the whole world, he erected it on that very spot.

From *101 Jewish Stories,* New York Board of Jewish Education

THE MAGIC RING

aladin, the great Sultan of the Moslems, summoned Nathan the Wise and said to him: "I've heard you are very wise and can answer any question put to you. I'd like to ask you this: There are three great religions in the world - Judaism, Christianity and Islam. Which of them is the true religion? Which one should a man choose for the right way of life? After all, there can be only one right way, isn't that so?"

Nathan the Wise answered him with the following story:

Many years ago there lived a man in an eastern country. He owned a very expensive ring which had a special power —whoever wore the ring would be loved by everyone. The man never removed the ring from his finger. When he was near death, he gave his most beloved son the ring. When his other sons saw the ring on the finger of their brother, they showed him great respect, even though he was the youngest.

As time passed, each father gave the ring to his most beloved son. In one generation, the ring passed into the hands of a man who loved his three sons equally. The father had a perplexing problem—to which of his sons should he give the ring? The father wanted to test the goodness and sincerity of his sons to help him make a decision. He saw that each possessed equal merit, wisdom and goodness. So, the father said to himself: "What shall I do? I will promise the ring to each of my sons, for they are all deserving."

As the years passed and the time of his death

approached, the worried father remembered he had promised the ring to each of his sons. Suddenly a good idea occurred to him. He called in a skillful goldsmith and said to him: "Make me two more rings just like this one. Make them so carefully patterned after the magic ring that no one will be able to distinguish the original from the copies."

The goldsmith did exactly as he was directed. When he returned the rings, a wonderful thing happened! Not even the father could distinguish the original magic ring from the two copies. The relieved father secretly called in each of his sons and gave him one of the rings. "You are chosen," said the father each time, "to be the carrier of this magic ring."

Each son rejoiced that he was given the magic ring, and that he was the most beloved of his father.

When the old man died, each of the sons put on his ring and went to the father's house. To their great surprise, they noticed identical rings on the fingers of the other two brothers. The surprise turned to anger, the anger to hatred, and the hatred resulted in bitter quarreling.

"You've done a terrible thing," each one said to the other. "Your ring is forged! Only the ring that I'm wearing is the true one, because my father gave it to me himself."

What were the brothers to do? They went to a judge who carefully listened to the arguments of each of the three brothers. This was his final decision: "These three rings are all alike—the same in appearance and shape. And no one can see enough difference among them to say: 'This one only is the original magic ring.' Now there is only one way to tell which is the true original. The brother who is most beloved of all, most respected by everyone—he is the one wearing the original magic ring. Therefore, go! Each one of you return to your own homes, and do your best to make yourself the most beloved by your actions and virtues. Then people will say: 'This one who acts the best, the wisest, and the most honorably —he is wearing the original magic ring!'"

From *101 Jewish Stories*, New York Board of Jewish Education

THE FIGS

king went out with his army to battle. On the way he saw an old man planting saplings for fig trees. The king asked the old man: "Tell me, how old are you? Your bent back and your trembling hands testify that you have reached some great age."

"You are right, your Highness," said the old man. "I am over one hundred years old!"

The astonished king then asked the old man: "How does it happen that a man as old as you should choose to be occupied in planting young sapling trees?"

"My dear king," replied the old man, "My task throughout my life has always been to plant. If I am fortunately spared by God, then I shall live to eat of this fig tree that I am planting. And if I am dead by the time this tree has grown and flourished, then at least my sons will eat of its fruit, just as in my youth I ate from the trees that my forefathers planted for my sake."

For three years, the king remained away in bitter wars which took him to distant lands, and then he returned home by the same road. There he saw the same old man, stooped and hunched even nearer to the ground, his trembling hands more shaky than ever, but still working. He was carrying a heaped harvest basket and it was filled with beautiful fruit, the first fruit of the fig trees he had planted three years before.

The old man bowed, approached the king and said: "I am the old man whom you saw standing in this very garden three years ago, planting this same fig tree from which I am now harvesting the first fruits. With joy I shall bring it to the Temple. God has been pleased to let me eat of its fruits. I bring you some of them, O king, taste them yourself!"

The king tasted the fruit, thanked the old man, and ordered his servants to fill the basket with gold pieces, as a reward for this man's faith in the future.

From *101 Jewish Stories,* New York Board of Jewish Education

SEVEN GOOD YEARS: NOW OR LATER

O nce there was a couple who were good and pious. They worked hard always, but they never prospered.

One day, as the man was out in the field, an old man appeared before him. The old man was Elijah the Prophet sent by God to reward the couple for their faith and hard work.

Elijah said to the man, "God will grant you seven good years. Do you want them now or at the end of your life?" The man replied that he had always relied on his wife's wisdom in such matters, so he must go and ask her. Elijah agreed.

The wife's answer was direct: "Take the seven good years now, for we've no idea when the last seven will be, and if we use the seven years well, we may be able to provide for the future."

When the man informed Elijah of his wife's choice, Elijah gave the man a bag of gold, told him to use it well. Then he promised to return in seven years to see how the couple was doing and reclaim the gold.

Throughout the seven years, the couple continued to work hard, only now they prospered. With each new bounty, they shared with the less fortunate and educated their children. They prospered even more. In fact, they had much more gold at the end of the seven years than they had started with. The more they had, the more they helped others.

When Elijah returned at the end of seven years, he smiled as he witnessed how well and generously the couple had used their wealth. He did not reclaim the original bag of gold, but left it with them to continue their good work.

Retold from traditional sources

THE FINDER'S REWARD

ever before had such good luck befallen the poor tailor! He was walking with his head bent down along the highway when suddenly his eyes spotted a wallet half hidden in a bush. To his great joy, the wallet contained 200 gold pieces.

But his joy was not to last long. That night the sexton announced in the synagogue that the richest man in town had lost a wallet full of gold pieces, and he begged the finder to return the wallet, according to the Law. A generous reward would be given.

All day long, the poor tailor wrestled with his conscience. "He can afford it," said his Evil Spirit, "and my wife and children are on the verge of starvation."

"No," said his Good Spirit, "the money is not yours, and the Torah commands that if a man finds property which does not belong to him, on the highway he must return it to its rightful owner."

With many sighs and groans, the poor tailor knocked at the door of the rich man's house, extended the well filled wallet to him with shaking and reluctant hands, and said, "Here is your wallet. My need is greater than yours, but I cannot break the Commandment. Take your money and give me any reward."

But the rich man thought to himself. "What a fool this man is to return such a large sum of money. Such an idiot deserves no reward. There's no reason for me to keep my promise." So he said: "Reward? You don't deserve any reward. There were three hundred gold pieces in the wallet I lost, and now I count only two hundred! You are a thief. You have already stolen 100 gold pieces of my property!"

"Is this my reward for my honesty—to be called a thief?" cried out the poor tailor. "You are a greedy miser and you shall pay the reward, like it or not!"

The next day, the poor tailor brought his protest before the rabbi. The two disputants stood before the rabbi while the rest of the town crowded around to hear the rabbi's judgment.

"You claim that this wallet contained three hundred gold pieces?" the rabbi asked the rich man, looking at him with piercing eyes—for his reputation as a miser was well known. "Yes," said the rich man, "and he returned to me a wallet containing only two hundred gold pieces," shrieked the old miser, "and in addition to stealing a hundred gold pieces, he also claimed the reward! Some nerve!"

"This wallet cannot be yours," said the rabbi. "The one you lost contained three hundred gold pieces, and the wallet this poor tailor found contained only two hundred gold pieces. Clearly then, the tailor found another wallet than the one you lost. And according to our Law, since the owner cannot be found, the property then reverts to the finder, and so I decree that it goes to the tailor. Case dismissed."

All the townspeople laughed and applauded the rabbi's one-sided but clever disposition of the case of the rich man who attempted to steal the little bit that belonged to the poor tailor. A promise must be kept!

From *101 Jewish Stories,* New York Board of Jewish Education

THE DISHONEST CARPENTER

 n a city in Spain lived a carpenter who was a fine craftsman and builder. He had one fault—greed. The mayor of the city knew what a fine carpenter and builder he was, and gave him many houses to build.

His plans and designs were beautiful, but he used cheap materials in the structure of the houses. The houses stood up very well, but he made extra profits because he did not put in the quality materials for which the city had paid.

After twenty years of such work, the mayor assigned him the task of building an especially beautiful private home. The mayor did not say for what specific purpose he wanted the house built. It would serve as a private dwelling for an honored citizen. By this time, the carpenter had grown very greedy. Again, the plan for the house was very beautiful. But the materials he put into the house were very poor indeed. You could not tell from the outside, however, because the architect made sure that the outside looked beautiful. When the house was finished, the mayor prepared a banquet and invited all the important people of the city to dedicate the house, and to make the presentation to the honored citizen who was to occupy it. At the banquet the mayor rose and made the following speech:

"For twenty years, our chief carpenter has served the city faithfully. And so the members of the city council decided to honor him. Therefore, we gave him a commission to build a private dwelling, as beautiful as could be made. We are happy at this moment to say: Dear carpenter, this house you have built, so beautiful and so enduring and strong, is yours, as a reward from our city for your long labors!"

From *101 Jewish Stories,* New York Board of Jewish Education

WINE TO THE WEDDING

 long time ago there was a king who had a daughter. When the time came for the daughter to be married, the king decided to invite the entire kingdom to the celebration. The only gift he asked of his people was that they each bring a bottle of wine from their own vineyards. The king planned that everyone would pour his own bottle of wine into a huge vat. At the appropriate moment, each person would toast the bride and groom with a glass of wine from the vat—the wine that was a blend of everyone's contributions.

On the day of the wedding, the people came bringing the bottles of wine and poured them into the vat as they entered the palace gardens. When it was time to begin the toast, the king turned on the spigot for the first glass of wine. A strange thing happened. What came out was a clear liquid— water! It seems that each of the people in the kingdom thought: "Why should I bring my good wine? Why, if I bring a bottle of water, no one will ever know. With thousands of bottles of wine, my bottle will hardly dilute the rest of the wine so it won't make any difference." But everyone had the same idea, and each brought only a bottle of water. Each person had made a difference.

From *Jewish Stories One Generation Tells Another* by Penninah Schram

THE FOX AS ADVOCATE

t so happened that the lion grew angry with all the animals for their disobedience, and they in their fear were looking for someone to plead their case. No one wanted the task except the fox, who offered his services gladly. "Come along with me," he told the other animals. "I know three hundred fables, and they will appease our king."

The animals were delighted, and they all set off to see the lion. After they had gone some distance, the fox suddenly stopped. "What has happened?" the animals asked anxiously.

"I have just forgotten a hundred fables," replied the fox. "No matter," said the other animals. "Two hundred will be plenty for the lion."

So they all set off again, but before long the fox stopped again. "Imagine," he said, looking ashamed, "I have forgotten another hundred fables."

"It can't be helped," the animals replied. "Anyway, you still have a hundred. Let's hurry, so the lion won't be even angrier with us."

Soon the animals were standing before the lion's den. A terrible growling came from inside, and the animals began to shake with fear. "An unfortunate thing has happened," whispered the fox. "I cannot remember a single fable. You will have to get along without me. Let everyone answer for his own faults, and speak as best he can!"

From *Jewish Folktales* by Leo Pavlat

TWO HUMBLE MEN

 abbi Jacob and Rabbi Israel went to a convention of rabbis that was held in a great city. When these two famous rabbis arrived, the Jews rushed to greet them with the honor and respect they deserved. They prepared a beautifully decorated carriage, drawn by two magnificent horses to bring the two rabbis to the gates of the city.

In their enthusiasm, several members of the welcoming committee unharnessed the horses to put themselves within the harness, in order to have the honor of pulling the two rabbis by their own strength. The two humble rabbis did not understand what was going on. Soon other Jews harnessed themselves in to help draw the decorated carriage.

Rabbi Jacob said to himself, "For whom is all this honor? It can only be for the great scholar, my friend Rabbi Israel, who is sitting here beside me. I must join in honoring him." So he got out of the carriage and joined the crowd that was pulling in harness. Because of the great multitude of cheering admirers, he was not recognized.

Rabbi Israel said to himself: "For whom is all this honor? It can only be for the great scholar, my friend Rabbi Jacob. I must join in honoring him." He too, jumped off the carriage seat and joined the crowd that was pulling in harness.

And so, the two humble rabbis assisted in pulling the empty carriage, while the crowd, unaware that the carriage was now empty, cheered the pious scholars.

From *101 Jewish Stories*, New York Board of Jewish Education

FORBIDDEN FRIENDSHIP

hey walked together near the olive trees at the border, hand in hand, grandmother and grandson. And when they stopped to rest, the little boy looked up at his grandmother and said, "People say that here the olives grow bigger and tastier than anywhere in the land and that the blossoms are the most beautiful on these olive trees. Why is that, Grandma?" "Well as with most important things, there's a reason, his grandmother replied. "And, I've been waiting for you to be old enough to tell you this story. You see, it is a true story. In fact, the story is about my father who told it to me when I was about your age, and he had brought me here for the first time."

When my father was a little boy, Israel was not yet a state, but the Arabs and the Jews were enemies and my father was not allowed to play down here near the border between the Jewish village and the Arab village. His parents forbade him to go near the Arab village, and my father was a good boy, so he listened. But one day, I guess his head was in the clouds, and his mind journeyed away. He crossed from his side of the village to the Arab side, and before he realized it, my father was surrounded by older Arab boys who began to tease and taunt him. Because he was very small and not sure of the language and afraid of both the boys and what his parents would say if they knew, my father began to cry. But the boys began to shout and continued to taunt him. And then through the crowd, my father heard someone yelling at the older boys to leave my father alone. The voice belonged to a small Arab boy and amazingly, the older boys listened to that little boy, and they stopped hurting my father. Now perhaps the older boys were tired, or perhaps they had achieved what they wanted, which was to get my father to cry. Whatever the reason, they left, and my father turned to the small Arab boy who had rescued him. The boy was wiry and frail, but feisty. He had hair as black as the raven's wing and dazzling black eyes that glistened in the sunlight. And the two boys looked at one another, and they smiled.

They played all that day, the games that all children play. They acted out scenes and adventures from their individual and mutual heritage. They re-created the heroes from their own cultures, and they told each other new words and shared games from their separate cultures. At day's end, the Arab boy asked my father to return the next day, and my father promised. And, he came back and he played. He returned the day after that and the day after that until, eventually, his mother asked him why he didn't play with his friends on his street and wanted to know where he went each day. My father was an honest boy, so he told her. She grew alarmed and told his father, and together they made him promise never to return to the Arab village, ever.

My father did promise that he would never go back, but he broke that promise—only once, for he was a good boy. But, he felt he had to go back and tell his friend why he could never return to play again. His friend understood. He knew that his parents would never allow him to go to the Jewish village if the situation were reversed. The boys played all that day. Before they said goodbye, they took the pits from the olives they had eaten with lunch, and in a gesture more symbolic than practical, with intuitiveness beyond their years, they sowed the seeds along the border, watered the earth and then said goodbye, forever. From those seeds these olive trees grew more beautiful, more fragrant and larger than anywhere in the land, a testimony to that forbidden friendship.

When his grandmother stopped, the boy thanked her for sharing the story and then he told her that he would like to come back to this place often, to what he now called his grandfather's olive grove. They rose together to leave. Hearing a noise, the boy turned and saw a small Arab boy who was wiry and frail, but feisty. He had hair as black as the raven's wing and dazzling black eyes that glistened in the sunlight.

The two boys looked at one another, and they smiled.

By Corinne Stavish, inspired by *The Secret Grove* by Barbara Cohen

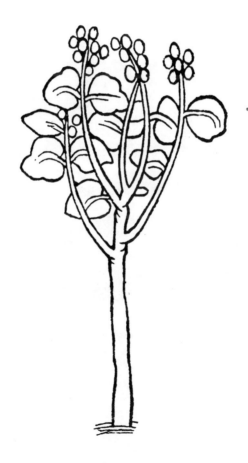

FEATHERS

nce there lived a woman who spoke negatively about all things and all people. She was disliked by most of the community, and because she had no friends, she spoke even more harshly about her neighbors. Her tongue was loose and wagged constantly. Much of what she said, people ignored. However, some of what she said was harmful and hurtful. The community grew outraged and complained to the rabbi.

The rabbi called the woman to him and said, "You must stop speaking the way you do about people. You have no idea how much damage you create."

"Nonsense, Rabbi," said the woman. "They are words only. First of all, they do not do damage. Secondly, I can take them back if you are so upset."

"Before you do anything," said the rabbi, " I want you to go home and get the biggest feather pillow you can. Next, cut it open and toss all the feathers to the wind. After that, come back to me."

The woman went home and did exactly as the rabbi instructed. Then, she returned to him. "Now," he directed, "get a new pillowcase and go and gather up all the feathers and bring back the new pillowcase, filled with them."

The woman left and returned hours later with only a few feathers in the pillowcase. "Well?" demanded the rabbi, "where is the filled pillowcase; where are all the feathers?"

The woman was sobbing. "Oh, Rabbi, I made such a mess; feathers were scattered everywhere, sticking in trees so I could not reach them, floating in the water. Feathers were everywhere making the village ugly, but, I could not retrieve most of them. Almost all of them flew away. I have no idea where to go to begin to gather them."

"Precisely," said the rabbi. "So it is with your evil words that are seemingly as light as those feathers. You have no idea where those words travel or what damage they do. You also can never find them to take them back. Do you understand?"

"Yes," the woman replied, sincerely. And, she changed her ways.

Retold from traditional sources

A BANQUET IN HEAVEN

righteous man was permitted by God to get a preview of the world to come. In a celestial place, he was ushered into a large room where he saw people seated at a banquet table laden with delicious food, but not a morsel had been touched. The righteous man gazed in wonder at the people seated at the table. They were hungry and wanted to eat—but did not!

"If they are hungry, why is it they don't eat and enjoy the food before them?" asked the righteous man.

"They cannot feed themselves," said his heavenly guide... "If you will notice, each has his arms strapped so that no matter how he tries, he cannot get the food into his mouth."

"Truly, this is hell," said the righteous one as they left the hall.

The heavenly attendant escorted him across the hall into another room, where the righteous man observed another beautiful table, equally laden with delicacies. Here, however, he noticed those seated around the table were well fed, happy and joyous. To his amazement, he saw these people also had their arms strapped.

He turned to his guide and asked: "How is it that they are so well fed even though they are unable to transport the food to their mouths?"

"Behold," said the heavenly guide. The righteous man looked on with wonder as he watched each one feeding his neighbor. The straps, he noticed, were tied to allow enough freedom for each individual to feed his neighbor, even though he was unable to feed himself.

"This is really heaven," said the righteous man.

"In truth it is," the guide answered. "As you can see, the difference between hell and heaven is a matter of cooperation—of serving one's fellow man."

From *101 Jewish Stories*, New York Board of Jewish Education

ON BEING TRUE TO ONE'S SELF...

hen Rabbi Mordecai died, his son, Rabbi Noah, became the next leader in the community. After a short time had passed, the leaders of the community came to the rabbi complaining about his decisions and religious leadership. They said: "We wanted you to take over your father's position because we thought you would do as your father did. You do not do as your father did. You have disappointed us."

Rabbi Noah replied: "I do exactly as my father did. He did not imitate, and I do not imitate."

hen Rabbi Zusya was dying, his disciples came to surround him. He told them that he was frightened. "Why are you frightened?" they asked. "When you get to the World to Come, you will be praised. Your hospitality is as great as Abraham's; your leadership parallels Moses'. What do you have to fear?"

"What I fear," replied Zusya, "is not that I will be asked, 'Zusya, why were you not more like Abraham? Why were you not more like Moses?' What I fear is that I will be asked, 'Zusya, why were you not more like Zusya?'"

Retold from Hasidic sources

CHOICES

nce there was a student who wanted to prove the teacher wrong. This student was tired of the teacher being right all the time.

One day, the student sat in the back of the room and called out to the teacher, "Since you always know the answer, tell me, is the baby bird I'm holding in my hand alive or dead?" The student held up a hand with a fist closed over the bird.

The student thought: "If the teacher says that the bird is alive, I will crush it to death. If the teacher says that the bird is dead, I will open my hand and the bird will fly away. In either event, the teacher will be wrong."

The teacher looked deeply into the student's eyes, into the student's heart, and into the student's soul. Then the teacher said, "As with all things, the choice is in your hands."

Retold from traditional sources

THE STONECUTTER

I n a time when wishing worked, there was a stone-cutter who would go each day with his pick and hew the stones from the mountain. He hated what he was and wanted to be the most powerful thing in the world. One day he heard the crowd roaring, and when he looked over the side of the mountain from which he was hewing stone, he saw a king being carried and hailed by the crowd.

"That's it," he thought. "If I were to be a king, then I would be cheered and hailed. I would be so powerful." So, he wished to be a king, and he became a king.

He loved being carried by the crowd and being cheered, but it was very hot out, and he was uncomfortable with all his furs and heavy crown. "What is it," he thought, "that is making me, the powerful king, so uncomfortable?" It was the sun.

"Oh, I should have wished to be the sun—it is more powerful than the king." So, he wished to be the sun, and he became the sun. He loved that. He could use his light to make things grow. Wherever he directed his rays, he was in control. But then, something more powerful crossed his path and blocked his light. It was a cloud.

"Oh, I should have wished to be a cloud—it is more powerful than the sun." So, he wished to be the cloud, and he became the cloud. He loved it. He could dart here, there and everywhere and block the sun. But then, something more powerful lifted him up and carried him off. It was the wind.

"Oh, I should have wished to be the wind—it is more powerful than the cloud." So, he wished to be the wind and he became the wind. He loved it. He could blow here and blow there and move whatever he wanted. How powerful he was. Until he tried to blow something over that could not be moved. It was a mountain.

"Oh, I should have wished to be the mountain—it is more powerful than the wind." So, he wished to be the mountain and he became the mountain. And he loved that. He was so powerful that he was indestructible. Nothing could move him. But wait, "Ouch! Oh no, what was it that was hurting the mountain?" It was the pick of the stonecutter!

Then he realized that the stonecutter was powerful. He then wished to be what he always had been. He became a stonecutter. Only this time, he understood his own power.

Retold from traditional sources

YOU CAN'T PLEASE EVERYBODY

 father and his son were traveling along a road, accompanied by their donkey. The father was riding on the donkey, and the son was walking by his side. They met a man who said to the father, "You ought to be ashamed of yourself. You have no pity for this poor young boy, making him walk while you ride."

The father dismounted and let his son ride the donkey.

Later they met a second man who said to the son, "Worthless youth, have you no pity for your poor old father?" So both he and the son got on the donkey together.

They met a third man who said, "Cruel people, have you no pity for this pitiful creature? Why make it support both of you?"

So the two of them got off and walked alongside the donkey.

Then, they met a fourth man, who laughed at them, "Three donkeys walking along together on the road, and none of them rides on the other donkey!"

The father and son looked at each other, wondering what they could do to please everybody. They found a solution. The two of them continued on foot as they carried the donkey on their backs.

From *101 Jewish Stories*, New York Board of Jewish Education

PRAYING WITH A FLUTE

 farmer had a son who was so slow and retarded in learning that he could not even learn to read the Hebrew alphabet. He did not know how to say his prayers and was not able to read the Siddur. His father never brought him among the congregation, because the boy did not understand what was going on in the synagogue. But on Yom Kippur, his father took him along to hear the services. Even though he understood so little, the father still thought that his son should take part in the High Holiday service of the Jewish people.

On the farm, one of the boy's tasks was to mind the cattle and sheep and to attend to the needs of the flocks. While he sat in the fields minding the animals he would play on a little wooden flute. He loved playing on his flute, and drew out of it beautiful and mournful melodies. The sheep loved the sounds of his sad melodies and they would follow the shepherd boy just to hear the notes he drew from the homemade instrument.

The boy took his flute along with him to the synagogue on Yom Kippur, and hid it in his coat. All day long, the boy sat quietly in the synagogue without praying. But when the time came for the Musaf Prayers, the boy whispered to his father: "Dear father, I want to play my flute." Angrily, the father shook him and scolded him. He warned him not to do such a sacrilegious thing on so holy an occasion as Yom Kippur. Once again at the afternoon service, Mincha, the boy begged, "Please, father, give me permission to play the flute." And when the father looked deep into the longing eyes of his beloved son, and saw how keenly he wanted to take part in the services of this Day of Atonement, his heart melted for him and he whispered: "Where is the flute?" Thinking his father would now give him permission to play his beloved instrument, the boy showed him in which pocket of his suit the flute was concealed. But the father wanted to prevent the boy from playing his flute, and he grabbed hold of the pocket and held it, for fear that the boy would play on it in the middle of the holy service.

Later, while the congregation was in prayer at the Nielah Service, the father arose to pray together with the congregation. Seeing his advantage, the boy withdrew from his father's grasp the pocket his father was clutching, and he drew out the flute and began playing on it the mournful shepherd melodies he had composed. The congregation listened, astonished. Everyone remained still. The services stopped.

And so, in the midst of the great Nielah Prayer, as the gates of heaven are said to be closing slowly upon the atoning people, to allow them a last chance for penitence, the mournful and heartbreaking flute played on. When he stopped, the rabbi arose before the congregation and spoke: "This child's flute spoke to God in a voice greater than our prayers. All day long God has been hearing our prayers. And in this boy's heart, although he did not know how to pray along with us in our customary way, there burned the desire to serve God with prayer. So strong was his desire that his prayer upon the flute went directly up to serve God. His innocent heart offered a prayer which God received more readily than he did our own prayers with words. The prayers of the innocent are mightier than all others."

From *101 Jewish Stories*, New York Board of Jewish Education

VENGEANCE IN VAIN

 bird who lived on the seashore decided to build a nest. When the tide was out one day, he set to work. He fetched twigs, feathers and dry leaves, but no sooner had he gathered together everything he needed, than the tide came in. The waves rolled up and soon washed away everything the little bird had so carefully collected. The bird was furious. "I swear I shall take revenge on the sea!" he cried, and at once set about it. He took a drop of sea water in his beak, flew ashore, and emptied the water onto the ground. Then he picked up a beakful of sand and flew back to the sea with it. He dropped the sand in the sea, and flew back and forth like that until the moon came out. After a few days of this work, the little bird was quite exhausted. He sat on the shore watching the waves roll in, impatient to get his strength back so he could continue. Then another bird came flying up and said to him: "I have been watching you for a long time, and I am sorry for you. You wish to have your revenge, but vengeance is a poor counselor. Try as you may, you will never destroy the sea. But if you go to work with good intentions, even a little labor will have its reward."

The bird took his new friend's advice and flew inland, where he soon built a fine nest.

From *Jewish Folktales* by Leo Pavlat

THE ALPHABET

n ignorant, impoverished peasant entered the synagogue for worship. He listened to the learned men, the scholars, and the experts chant their beautiful prayers to God. Since, he too, wished to express his love of God, he ascended before the pulpit and stood before the Holy Ark. Over and over again he repeated the letters of the alphabet, in a voice full of feeling and reverence: "Aleph, bet, gimel..., aleph, bet gimel..." and so forth, his voice almost choking with emotion. The scholars and the sages in the congregation were astonished to hear this rustic and unlearned countryman repeating the letters of the Hebrew alphabet over and over again.

They nudged one another, commenting on this man's ignorance. They laughed at him. They ridiculed his mannerisms, his uncouth accent, his ragged appearance.

"Why, just listen," said the one with the most pointed beard and the most highly arched eyebrows, "he doesn't even know the simplest prayers of the Sabbath service!"

But finally the peasant began to speak, and their laughter died in their throats. Their mockery turned to shame, as they heard his prayer to God, which issued out of the deepest chambers of his heart: "Lord of the Universe, I am a simple man, an ignorant man. Oh, how I wish that I had the words to fashion beautiful prayers to You. But alas! I cannot find the words. So, listen to me, O God, as I recite the letters of the alphabet. I'm sure that You know what I think and feel. Take these letters of the alphabet, dear God, and You, Yourself form and shape the words which express the yearning, the love for You, that is in my heart."

And now the scoffers bowed their heads in shame as the

unlearned peasant again repeated, with tears filling his eyes, the letters of the alphabet over and over: "Aleph, bet, dear God of the Universe, gimel, daled, O most compassionate God..."

From *101 Jewish Stories,* New York Board of Jewish Education

THE PRINCESS AND RABBI JOSHUA

 abbi Joshua, the son of Hananyah, was extremely learned, but he was unfortunately also a very ugly man. Some children would even be frightened by looking at him. But his great learning, wit, and wisdom had won him even the respect of the Emperor Trajan. Once, while he was at the court, one of the princesses laughed at him for his ugliness.

"How is it," she said, "that such glorious wisdom is enclosed in so common–looking a face?"

The rabbi was not dismayed by her words and he said to her: "Tell me, Princess, in what kind of vessels does your father keep his fine wines?"

"Why, in earthen vessels, of course," said the princess. "Everybody keeps them in jars made out of the earth, don't they?"

"Everybody?" said the Rabbi. "True, ordinary people do but an emperor's wine ought to be kept in more precious vessels."

The princess thought he was in earnest. She ordered a number of containers of the emperor's fine wines be emptied out of their earthen jars and put into gold and silver vessels. To her great surprise she soon discovered what everyone else knew—if fine wine is kept in metal vessels, no matter how precious the metal, it soon gets sour and becomes unfit to drink.

The next time she saw Rabbi Joshua, the princess scoffed at him and said: "Very fine advice, indeed, you have given me. Do you know that the precious wine is now sour and spoiled?"

"Then you should be convinced," said the Rabbi, "that wine keeps best in plain and common vessels. It is the same with wisdom and knowledge."

"But," argued the princess, "I know many persons who are both wise and handsome."

"That may be true," replied the learned scholar, "but they would probably be even wiser, if they were less handsome."

From *101 Jewish Stories,* New York Board of Jewish Education

THE HONORED GARMENT

zariah and his wife were poor, but not unhappy, for they were kind, honest, and respected by their neighbors.

When their son was born, everyone brought gifts. A relative sent them a few yards of the most expensive and beautiful material in the world. The wife locked it away and said, "When my son is a man, I will send him out into the world in a wonderful robe made of this material."

The baby grew into a sweet and smart boy, but because they were poor, he was always dressed in ragged clothing.

One day a rich merchant invited everyone in town to a feast. Among the guests was Azariah's son, now grown. But nobody made room for him at the table, nor did they invite him to eat. Feeling rejected, the boy went home and told his mother what had happened.

"Don't be unhappy," said his mother. "Wait, and I'll finish a robe I am making for you that is so beautiful, everyone will bow down to you."

So the mother finished the robe she was making from the material they had received when the boy was born.

The boy went back to the feast, now dressed in the finest of robes. And as soon as the rich man saw him he got up, bowed before the boy, and said, "Come sit beside me, and eat and drink as much as you like."

The boy sat, took off his magnificent robe, and held the robe over the food. "Eat, robe," he said. "Eat all you want."

Everyone was startled. The rich man asked, "Why are

you talking to your robe?"

The boy replied, "the first time I came to your feast, I was dressed in tattered clothing. Then you paid no attention to me. Nobody asked me to sit down and eat. But when I arrived in my fancy outfit, you treated me royally. That's why I told my robe to eat. It was my wonderful clothes, not me, you were happy to see. So to me, even the sweetest thing on your table tastes bitter.

At that, the boy left and went back to his humble but proud home, and the rich man was ashamed, for he knew that the boy was right.

From *One Minute Jewish Stories* by Shari Lewis

DISCUSSION GUIDE

iscussing a story is not about finding the right answer, but about sharing ideas and attitudes. Whether stories are told in small groups, led by experienced facilitators, or shared around a family table, no one should impose meaning on the story. Each person is entitled to see what he/she can in the story. Communication and understanding are the goals, not correcting. (See introductory notes about dialogue).

What follows are some general suggestions for using the story in a discussion, as well as, specific ideas for two of the stories in the book. The questions and process can be modified for any of the stories in this collection or any other. They are not the only questions, but a good way of beginning. Be prepared for people not to answer questions. It may be the mood of the group; it may be that the story is not the right one for the group. Either is fine. Whatever happens, do not tell the group what the story should mean—that is an individual choice. One can always say what the story means to oneself, but not to anyone else.

1. Tell the story.

Try not to read the story word for word. One person in the group can retell the story, or the entire group/family can reconstruct the tale by taking turns as they remember specifics. The purpose here is not to "perform" the story but to make certain that everyone knows what happens in the story. There is no "correct" language because the story was TOLD from generation to generation. Do not worry about the exact words. You will honor the story by repeating the events and the tone/intention of the tale.

In the story "The Two Brothers," the plot is easy to

learn because of the traditional repetition of threes. The language is simple as are the events, so it should be easy.

In the story "Noah," the language is more complex and the sequence is more difficult to remember. (Hint: The animals are listed alphabetically in the sequence: ewe lamb, lion, monkey, pig.)

2. Let people react. (Do not hurry this process.)

A good story, no matter how short, should just wait while people digest it for a few minutes. This is the time to observe people's expressions. Do people look interested, pleased, angry, bored, excited, eager, confused, etc.?

If people do not like the story or think it is stupid or boring, do not apologize or get defensive. Remind them that you did not write the story and you would appreciate it if they do not "kill the messenger." Blame the editor.

3. Discuss reactions.

Ask members of the group/family how the story made them feel. (Happy, sad, angry, apathetic, compassionate, silly, defensive, etc.) Did they like the story? Why? Why not? Be prepared (and tolerant) for many varied responses. We all "feel" differently about things, so never say, "Well you should not feel that way; that is not what the story is about." Rather, say, "Well, that is different from what I thought, and I'd like to think more about your reaction. Let's talk more."

With the story, "Noah" people usually laugh at the image of a person being foolishly drunk and also enjoy the cleverness of the riddle. This story is a good example of a midrash, a story that expands biblical text. It is also a morality tale and rather blatant in its message. Today's young people might not like how obvious the message is. The point to emphasize is that excess is an age-old problem that affected even one as righteous as Noah.

4. Ask: If you could be one character in the story, which one

would it be? Why?

This question always leads to a very dynamic interchange. It stimulates much discussion because it involves choice, but limited choice. We're not asking, "if you could be anyone, who would it be," but within the story, who appeals to you?" An effective strategy is first to list all of the characters. Remember that inanimate objects and animals are also characters.

In the story "The Two Brothers," the obvious character choices are the two brothers. However, remind the group/family that the father is very important in this story—he leaves the property. Also, what about the wife and the four children? And, let's not forget King Solomon. In fact, the wheat is almost a character in this story and can certainly be discussed as the "offering" each brother gives. (In a session I once led at B'nai B'rith Youth's International Leadership Training Conference in Starlight, PA for teens from around the world, a group concluded that they, the children of the 90's were the "offering" their parents were making in the same manner that Abraham had "offered Isaac as a sacrifice." The altar of sacrifice now, the teens concluded, is divorce.)

In the story "Noah," neither Noah, Satan, any of the animals, nor the vineyard is a positive choice. This leads to exactly the kind of discussion you want with teens. Good questions here are: "Who is responsible for the vineyard, its product and its use?" "Since drinking has been abused historically, what are some solutions?" (Be prepared for someone noticing that Satan not only comments on people's foolishness but warns against drinking. Can one associated with evil sometimes be an ally in disguise? Can we learn from the mistakes of others?)

As with all discussions, the leader/facilitator/parent does not have to worry about what to answer. Listening is a very important part of this interchange. It is always prudent to say "I want to give this more thought" rather than to say something you might regret later. Then give it more thought.

5. Continue: Which character would you not want to be? Why?

The comments above are relevant here. The discussion gets to be even more interesting because some negative reactions get noted.

In the story "The Two Brothers," the reactions might focus on which brother NOT TO BE, married or unmarried. Ask: Does one of these brothers have greater need than the other? What would you do if you were one of the brothers? Be aware that sometimes younger children will say that they don't want to be the father because he died. Some will want to be King Solomon because he is powerful. All of these choices are legitimate and can always be followed with the questions, "Why?" or "Can you tell us more?"

In the story "Noah," most people do not want to be anyone in the story. That is a good starting point for a discussion on how to avoid being the characters in the story.

6. Ask: How would you change the story if you could?

This is one of the meatier issues for most groups. People love to discuss how they would change things, assuming that their changes will be improvements. With this discussion, unbridled imaginations soar, and you can easily stray away from the "ideas" of the story, but a great deal of humor and fun result. If you're not sure what to do here, just remember two things: 1) What is your goal for the discussion and 2) What is important in the story. As long as you honor both, you cannot do the "wrong" thing. Remember, the story of Joseph and his brothers is now told as a rock musical, but the intent of the story remains. However, sometimes the changes people suggest make the original story collapse.

In the story "The Two Brothers," there are many changes your group/family may suggest. Frequently young people want to change the premise that the brothers share equally. This is a good discussion point. You might ask: What is the source for the brothers sharing everything "equally?"

Most people assume that it is a dictate of the father. However, after you discuss the "wisdom" of sharing equally, and before you let people make that change in the story, ask them what happens to the storyline if the brothers do not have to share equally. The answer is that the story falls apart. Therefore, that is not a change that can be made. However, a change we can make is to add a scene before the "sharing" such as the "reading of the will" or a deathbed scene with the father where the brothers learn together that they must divide everything equally. This heightens the family drama and adds a potential discussion about sibling rivalry.

In the story "Noah," people usually want to change the last line. That, however, changes the facts in the story, so we can't do that. This is a good place to have a discussion about learning from the examples of others or from one's own mistakes. A change that can be made, and adds to the depth of the discussion, is to ask what other animals might be represented in the story? For example, might one of the animals be a "stiff-necked giraffe?"

7. Have the group "act out" or re-create the story.

This activity is not only a great deal of fun, but people can also "see" the story and many discussion points get amplified and relationships are much clearer because of the physical aspect. Also, people get away from the pressure of "sharing feelings" and let themselves go while dramatizing a story. The results are much more intense and unguarded.

With the story "The Two Brothers," dramatization is easy because the story is so visual. Frequently with this story, people act out the scene about how the brothers stacked the wheat, adding thoughts about the happiness the brothers gave each other. (This is a good time to remind people that Judaism teaches that the highest form of giving is anonymously.)

With the story "Noah," the dramatization can get hilarious with different people playing the animals. When young people see how ridiculous drunkenness looks, they will laugh. Ask them if this is how they want to look.

8. Ask: To whom would you want to tell this story?

Choosing an audience to tell the story to shows what people think about the story, how they treasure it, and what the importance of the story is. For example, if they don't care about whom they tell the story to, they might not care about the story. If teens want to tell the story to friends, it is a sure sign that it's an important story.

"The Two Brothers," is a story younger people usually want to share with family members. I've always seen that as a desire to have or to promote selfless love as the story demonstrates.

With the story "Noah," teens will usually want to share the story (mostly the clever riddle) with other teens. They do not want to share this story with adults because it gives the adults ammunition. Remind them that you did not write the story.

9. Ask: How would the story be different if it were set today ?

The question challenges people to think about how the story applies to their lives. Sometimes people end up making parodies of the story, which is just fine because they're dealing with the story.

In the story "The Two Brothers," the brothers today may not be farmers dividing wheat, but might be jewelers or car salesmen or any number of professions that could make the story very humorous without destroying its meaning. But then, we wouldn't have King Solomon in the story, so we'd have to ask, "What could we build today on that sacred spot?" In other words, "where's the holiness in our world today; who is the leader who would implement it?" Remember that the story takes place in Jerusalem. This could lead to a very interesting discussion about Israel and the importance of sacred spaces today.

In the story "Noah," Satan usually becomes some sort of mob leader or drug dealer when young people reset the story. Noah may become younger, a teenager, and all sorts of interesting dialogue results. Here is the time when teens want to change the ending of the story in the hope of being able to resist alcohol. And here, I let them do it.

10. Suggest that someone retell the story.

This is an excellent activity to summarize and/or conclude the discussion. The final telling will emphasize many points of the discussion. Do not hesitate to have the group retell the story in round robin. Someone starts the story and each person adds a bit to it until it is retold by the group and can be very satisfying since it reviews emotionally all the points of the discussion.

The most important thing to remember for all aspects of the discussion is to enjoy yourself. These stories are meant to trigger ideas and emotions. Most of all, they are meant to enjoy, to remember, to tell. They are seeds of ideas that we plant so that generations from now the fruits will continue to flourish.

SOURCES FOR JEWISH STORIES.... A BEGINNING

Ausubel, Nathan, ed. *A Treasury of Jewish Folklore.* New York: Crown Publishers, 1948.

Bialik, Hayim Nahman and Yehoshua Hana Ravnitzky, eds. *The Book of Legends, Sefer Ha-Aggadah.* New York: Schocken Books, 1992.

Board of Jewish Education of Greater New York. *101 Jewish Stories.* New York: BJE, 1961.

Frankel, Ellen. *The Classic Tales: 4,000 Years of Jewish Lore.* Northvale: Jason Aronson, 1989.

Freehof, Lillian. *Bible Legends: An Introduction to Midrash.* New York: UAHC Press, 1987 (3 volumes).

Gellman, Marc. *Does God Have a Big Toe?* New York: Harper & Row, 1989.

Ginzberg, Louis. *The Legends of the Jews.* Philadelphia: JPS, 1925 (7 volumes).

Goldstein, David. *Jewish Folklore and Legend.* London: The Hamlyn Publishing Group Ltd., 1980.

Hollender, Betty. *Bible Stories for Little Children.* New York: UAHC, 1955, RE 1986.

Lewis, Shari. *One Minute Jewish Stories.* New York: Doubleday, 1989.

Nahmad, N. M. *A Portion in Paradise and Other Folktales.* New York: W. W. Norton & Co., 1970.

Pavlat, Leo. *Jewish Folktales.* Prague: Greenwich House; distributed by Crown Publishers, 1986.

Rush, Barbara. *The Book of Jewish Women's Tales.* Northvale, Jason Aronson, 1994.

Schram, Penninah. *Jewish Stories One Generation Tells Another.* Northvale: Jason Aronson, 1987.

Schwartz, Howard. *Elijah's Violin and Other Jewish Fairy Tales.* New York: Harper & Row, 1983.

—— *Gabriel's Palace: Jewish Mystical Tales.* New York: Oxford University Press, 1993.

—— *Gates to the New City.* New York: Avon, 1983.

—— *Lilith's Cave.* San Francisco: Harper & Row, 1987.

Sewer, Blanche. *Let's Steal the Moon.* Boston: Little Brown, 1970.

Singer, Isaac B. *Stories for Children.* New York: Farrar, Straus, & Giroux, 1984.

Tenenbaum, Samuel. *The Wise Men of Chelm.* New York: Collier Books, 1975.

Wiesel, Elie. *Messengers of God: Biblical Portraits and Legends.* New York: Random House, 1976.

BOOKS ABOUT STORYTELLING

Baker, Augusta and Ellin Greene. *Storytelling: Art and Technique.* New York: Bowker Press, 1977.

Bauer, Caroline Feller. *Handbook for Storytellers.* Chicago: Chicago American Library Association, 1977.

Bettelheim, Bruno. *The Uses of Enchantment.* New York: Alfred A. Knopf, 1976.

Chambers, Dewey. *Storytelling and Creative Drama.* Dubuque: Wm. C. Brown, 1970.

Livo, Norma and Sandra Reitz. *Storytelling Activities.* Littleton CO: Libraries Unlimited, Inc., 1987.

Pellowski, Anne. *The World of Storytelling.* New York: B. R. Bowker, 1977.

Sawyer, Ruth. *The Way of the Storyteller.* New York: Viking Press, 1942.

Schimmel, Nancy. *Just Enough to Tell a Story: A Sourcebook for Storytelling,* 2nd Ed. Berkeley, CA. Sisters Choice Press, 1982.

Shedlock, Marie. *The Art of the Storyteller.* New York: D. Appleton & Co., 1916.

Wagner, Joseph. *Children's Literature Through Storytelling.* Dubuque: Wm. C. Brown & Co., 1970.

ABOUT THE EDITOR
CORINNE STAVISH

orinne Stavish of Southfield, Michigan has been a freelance storyteller and workshop leader for over fifteen years. She is a regular workshop leader at CAJE (Conference for Alternatives in Jewish Education) and travels throughout the country to teach and perform. National reviews of her three audio-cassette tapes applaud her style and material. A published author of stories and articles, Corinne is a faculty member in the Department of Humanities at Lawrence Technological University.

THE B'NAI B'RITH CENTER FOR JEWISH IDENTITY

T he B'nai B'rith Center for Jewish Identity (CJI) represents B'nai B'rith's commitment to providing opportunities and experiences to strengthen Jewish identity. Our mission is to enhance the transmission of Jewish values, ethics and knowledge from generation to generation; and to reach out to all members of the community including, but not limited to, the intermarried and the unaffiliated.

Our goals are to create and pilot various local programs and services, through the Center; to assist the Regional Centers in identifying which of the piloted programs to incorporate and how to tailor them to the individual needs of their communities; and to develop local programs that will be highly visible, substantive, well organized, and professional, to enhance positive Jewish experiences, and to reinforce the joy and relevancy of being Jewish.